The Things I **Love** About
Bedtime

Trace Moroney

The Five Mile Press

I **love** bedtime,
and these are things
I love most . . .

I have a bath,

brush my teeth . . .

and put on my favourite pyjamas.

Mum pretends she is a
huggle-monster
and chases me into bed,
and gives me a
great . . . **big**
. . . **hug!**

I snuggle into bed with
my teddy-bunny and
Dad reads me a story.

Then, we talk about the
best moments of my day . . .

like, building a
tree-hut together . . .

or, drawing
a really good
picture
for Mum,

or, playing fun games
with my friends.

Remembering my **best moments**
makes me feel good about being me!

Then, Dad always says . . .

Of all the
millions and squillions
of little bunnies around
the world, how did I get so
lucky to have the best one?
Goodnight, my
little snuggle-bunny.
I love you.

This makes me feel **really** special.

I close my sleepy eyes . . . and
think of all the things
I would like to dream about . . .

like, riding on a giant bumblebee
right up to the moon and back . . .

or, sailing in a pirate ship
on a sea of raspberry jam
and goldfish . . .

or, perhaps . . . just in my own bed . . .
feeling warm, safe and loved!

I **love** bedt . . i . . z z z z z z z

Notes for Parents and Caregivers

'The Things I Love' series shares simple examples of creating **positive thinking** about everyday situations our children experience.

A positive attitude is simply the inclination to generally be in an optimistic, hopeful state of mind. Thinking positively is not about being unrealistic. Positive thinkers recognise that bad things can happen to pessimists and optimists alike – however, it is the positive thinkers who *choose* to focus on the hope and opportunity available within every situation.

Researchers of positive psychology have found that people with positive attitudes are more creative, tolerant, generous, constructive, successful and open to new ideas and new experiences than those with a negative attitude. Positive thinkers are happier, healthier, live longer, experience more satisfying relationships, and have a greater capacity for love and joy.

I have used the word **love** numerous times throughout each book, as I think it best describes the *feeling* of living in an optimistic and hopeful state of mind, and it is a simple but powerful word that is used to emphasise our positive thoughts about people, things, situations and experiences.

Bedtime

Spending time with your child as they prepare for bed, and sleep, is a wonderful opportunity to develop and maintain a close and loving bond.

Playing a fun bedtime game, sharing a story, listening to them recount their favourite moments of the day, discussing dreams and future events they are looking forward to, praising them for a task well done (or good behaviour), and telling them how much you love them – all of these things create an environment in which your child will feel happy, safe, secure, loved and valued.

Ultimately, these simple rituals contribute to an increase in the positive emotion of your child. For you as the parent this is *precious* time in which you can be consciously and constructively involved in building a positive state of mind. Your child will hopefully internalise this optimism and it will guide them on a path to a full and happy life.

Sweet dreams little snuggle-bunnies!
Trace Moroney

For my son Matt,
I am honoured and blessed to be the one
to tuck you into bed every night,
and help you feel warm, safe, and loved.
xxx

The Five Mile Press Pty Ltd
1 Centre Road, Scoresby
Victoria 3179 Australia
www.fivemile.com.au
Part of the BonnierPublishing Group
www.bonnierpublishing.com
Illustrations and text copyright © Trace Moroney
All rights reserved
www.tracemoroney.com
First published 2009
This edition 2013
Printed in China 5 4 3 2 1
National Library of Australia Cataloguing-in-Publication entry
Moroney, Trace
The things I love about bedtime / Trace Moroney.
9781742114873 (hbk.)
9781742116815 (pbk.)
For pre-school age.
Bedtime--Juvenile literature.
649.6